The Squawking talking parrot

Written by
Janine Scott

Illustrated by
Deborah Rigby

www.autumnchildrensbooks.co.uk

Penelope Pirate wanted to teach her pet parrot, Polly, to talk.

"Let's start at the beginning of the alphabet. Repeat after me," said Penelope. "Angela and her awful aardvark, Angus, ate apples from Argentina!"

But Polly Parrot shut her beak and didn't try to speak.

So Penelope Pirate decided to join her pirate friends. They'd know what to do with a parrot that didn't talk.

Penelope put Polly in a bright blue boat and paddled to the balmy Bahamas.

"Blimey, that budgie's got birdbrain-itis!" bellowed a big, bold buccaneer when he saw the bird.

But Polly Parrot shut her beak and didn't try to speak.

The captain's cockatoo, Colin, called the crew over to check out Polly, who had crept into a corner to quietly count creepy-crawly crickets.

"Crikey!" cried the crew. "That crow's got cuckoo-itis!"

But Polly Parrot shut her beak and didn't try to speak.

As day dawned, the pirate captain had an idea.

"Let's dangle that dim-witted ducky in the dungeon till dinner time. That will make her talk."

"Definitely don't do that!" cried Penelope. "That's dastardly and dangerous!"

So the eager captain had to think
of another plan. Before long, he got
an encyclopedia and read everything
beginning with E to Polly Parrot.

Then, east of the equator, the captain made Polly sit an exam. She made eighty-eight errors in eighteen minutes.

"Eeekkk, you've got emptyhead-itis!" exclaimed the captain.

The captain was frightfully furious.
No pirate bird had ever failed before.

"That fowl's got featherbrain-itis!" cried
the fiery captain. "There's only one thing
for it. Let's go to a far-off frontier and find
a fix-it tree."

The captain and Penelope Pirate grabbed Polly.
They glided past glaciers in their goatskin kayak.

"Golly," gasped the captain. "I am a galloping goat!
I've guessed why Polly's gone gaga.
This goose has got goofy goon-itis!"

But Polly Parrot shut her beak
and didn't try to speak.

In a haze on the horizon, Penelope Pirate saw Hermit Haven, an island that is very hush-hush. Only pirates have heard of it. So Penelope, the captain and Polly hopped ashore and ate hundreds of fix-it fruits from the fix-it trees. But that didn't help Polly at all.

"That hen's got harebrain-itis!" hissed the hysterical captain. "Come on, hawk. TALK!"

But Polly Parrot shut her beak
and didn't try to speak.

Then they left the island in an instant. Penelope and the captain played *I Spy* while Polly idly watched icebergs inch their way into icy inlets.

But Polly Parrot shut her beak
and didn't try to speak.

After that, Penelope and the captain sang
jolly jingles on their journey back to the jetty.

"By jingo! That jay bird's got jittery-itis!
It just won't talk," joked the captain.

But Polly Parrot shut her beak
and didn't try to speak.

So they anchored the boat, and the captain
said kindly, "I'd keep that kookaburra
under lock and key!"

Then he kissed Penelope goodbye. "Just kidding,
kiddo!" he cried. "That kookaburra's kooky
but cute!"

Before long, as Penelope kayaked past
a kingfisher kingdom, Polly kept cackling,
making quite a kerfuffle.

Polly lisped: "I've said very little – a little less than a little – but I really don't have lamebrain-itis. I still like to squawk and I'd just love to talk if it weren't for this laryngitis!"

Then Polly Parrot shut her beak and didn't try to speak.

The Pirate picnic

Written by
Janine Scott

Illustrated by
Deborah Rigby

Penelope Pirate and Polly Parrot were sailing in the Pacific. All morning they had been painting the ship's planks purple. They were particularly pooped.

"I'm peckish," said Penelope Pirate.
"Let's pause and have a pirate picnic."

Penelope Pirate and Polly Parrot peeked
in the pantry at all the pleasant food.
They carried piles and piles of picnic food
up on to the deck.

Then Penelope Pirate put piles of food on to
plates and plonked them on a pink picnic rug.

"What can I pass you, Polly Parrot?" asked
Penelope Pirate. "Would you like pancakes,
pasta, pears, peas, pies, pineapple or plums?"

Polly Parrot just pouted and said,
"I don't want to appear rude,
but that's particularly unpleasant food."

Penelope Pirate went pale. She paused
and then pleaded, "Would you like parsley,
parsnips, passion fruit, pickles, pizza, popcorn
or pumpkin?"

Polly Parrot just pouted and said,
"I don't want to appear rude,
but that's particularly unpleasant food."

Penelope Pirate pretended to be polite,
but she was losing her pirate patience.
She paused and then pleaded, "Would you like
pastries, pawpaw, peaches, peanuts, pecans or
periwinkles?"

Polly Parrot peered at the food and pulled
a peculiar face. Penelope Pirate looked
particularly puzzled.

Polly Parrot paused and pondered and then said politely, "Pardon me for being so picky. I would prefer something pleasantly plain, pretty please. Polly just wants a cracker!"

Penelope Pirate perked up. She placed piles
of plain crackers on Polly Parrot's plate.

Polly Parrot was particularly pleased!

Ideas for Parents

- Reading with children is an important way of encouraging a love of books. It familiarises your child with the patterns of the written language and helps increase his or her vocabulary, assisting him or her on the road to literacy.

- Urge your child to join in with reading. Encourage him or her to finish sentences, try new words and read sections on his or her own. Always read the book a number of times. Repetition familiarises children with language patterns and makes it more likely that they will join in.

- Children learn best when an experience is enjoyable, so always make reading together a positive and fun experience.

Helping Children to Understand the Text and Build Reading Skills

The Squawking Talking Parrot

- Discuss the illustrations.

- Discuss and enjoy the alliteration used in the story. Note the repetitive use of the letters *p*, *a*, *b* and so on. Note how the author cleverly takes the reader through various letters of the alphabet. Help your child to identify some of these letters.

- There are many words in this book that will expand a child's vocabulary, such as: *dastardly, dangerous, hysterical, horizon*. Discuss the meaning of any unfamiliar words with your child.

- Discuss the way the story ends.

The Pirate Picnic

- Enjoy the alliteration used in the story. Together, identify some of the words that begin with the letter *p* and say them out loud together.

- Discuss any unfamiliar words with your child, such as: *unpleasant, pouted*.

- Discuss the way the story ends.